This edition published 1995 by Geddes & Grosset Ltd,
David Dale House, New Lanark, Scotland

Illustrated by Lyndsay Duff in the style of Charles Robinson

ISBN 1 85534 535 8

Printed in Slovenia

Tom, Tom, the Piper's Son

Mother Goose Rhymes

Tom, Tom, the Piper's Son

TOM, THE PIPER'S SON

Tom, Tom, the piper's son,
Stole a pig and away he run!
The pig was eat and Tom was beat,
And Tom went howling down the street.

PEG

Peg, Peg, with a wooden leg,
  Her father was a miller;
He tossed the dumpling at
    her head,
  And said he could not
    kill her.

A DIFFICULT RHYME

What is the rhyme for
  porringer?
The king he had a
  daughter fair,
And gave the Prince
  of Orange her.

THE OLD WOMAN TOSSED IN A BASKET

There was an old woman tossed up in a basket

Seventeen times as high as the moon;

Where she was going I couldn't but ask it,

For in her hand she carried a broom.

"Old woman, old woman, old woman," quoth I,

"Where are you going to up so high?"

"To brush the cobwebs off the sky!"

"May I go with thee?" "Aye, by-and-by."

POOR OLD ROBINSON CRUSOE

OOR old Robinson Crusoe!
Poor old Robinson Crusoe!
They made him a coat
Of an old nanny goat,
  I wonder why they could
    do so!
With a ring a ting tang,
And a ring a ting tang,
Poor old Robinson Crusoe!

TWO LITTLE DOGS

Two little dogs sat by the fire,
  Over a fender of coal-dust;
When one said to the other dog,
  " If Pompey won't talk, why,
    I must."

SATURDAY. SUNDAY

On Saturday night
    Shall be all my care
To powder my locks
    And curl my hair.

On Sunday morning
    My love will come in,
When he will marry me
    With a gold ring.

THE OWL IN THE OAK

THERE was an owl lived
in an oak,
    Whiskey, whaskey,
    weedle;
And all the words he ever
spoke
    Were fiddle, faddle, feedle.

A sportsman chanced to come that way,
    Whiskey, whaskey, weedle;
Says he, "I'll shoot you, silly bird,
    So fiddle, faddle, feedle!"

GEORGY PORGY

Georgy Porgy, pudding and
    pie,
Kissed the girls and made
    them cry.
When the boys came out to
    play,
Georgy Porgy ran away.

TO MARKET

To market, to market,
  To buy a fat pig;
Home again, home again,
  Jiggety jig.

To market, to market,
  To buy a fat hog;
Home again, home again,
  Jiggety jog.

THE LITTLE GUINEA-PIG

There was a little Guinea-Pig,
Who, being little, was not big;
He always walked upon his feet,
And never fasted when he eat.

When from a place he ran away,
He never at that place did stay;
And while he ran, as I am told,
He ne'er stood still for young or old.

He often squeak'd and sometimes vi'lent,
And when he squeak'd he ne'er was silent:
Though ne'er instructed by a cat,
He knew a mouse was not a rat.

One day, as I am certified,
He took a whim, and fairly died;
And, as I'm told by men of sense,
He never has been living since.

A
NICK AND A NOCK

A nick and a nock,
A hen and a cock,
And a penny for my master.

PANCAKE DAY

Great A, little A,
This is pancake day;
Toss the ball high,
Throw the ball low,
Those that come after
May sing heigh-ho!

HUSH·A·BYE·BABY

HUSH-
a-bye,
baby,

On the
tree top,

When the
wind blows,

The cradle
will rock;

When the bough breaks,
The cradle will fall,

Down tumbles baby,
Cradle, and all.

IN MARBLE HALLS

I N marble halls as white as milk,
    Lined with a skin as soft as silk;

Within a fountain crystal clear,
    A golden apple doth appear;

No doors there are to this strong-
    hold,
Yet thieves break in and steal the
    gold.

JACK SPRAT'S PIG

Jack Sprat had a pig, who was not very little,
    Nor yet very big;

He was not very lean, he was not very fat;

He'll do well for a grunt,
Says little Jack Sprat.

ROBIN-A-BOBIN

Robin-a-Bobin
   Bent his bow,
Shot at a pigeon,
   And killed a crow.

BANDY-LEGS

As I was going to sell
   my eggs,
I met a man with bandy
   legs;
Bandy legs and crooked
   toes,
I tripped up his heels,
   and he fell on his
   nose.

A APPLE PIE

A Apple Pie

A was an apple pie

B bit it,

C cut it,

D dealt it,

E eat it,

F fought for it,

G got it,

H had it,

J joined it,

K kept it,

L longed for it,

M mourned for it,

N nodded for it,

O opened it,

P peeped in it,

Q quartered it,

R ran for it,

S stole it,

T took it,

V viewed it,

W wanted it,

X Y Z and all wished a piece of it

THE PUMPKIN EATER

Peter, Peter, pumpkin eater,
Had a wife and could n't keep
    her;
He put her in a pumpkin shell,
And there he kept her very
    well.

HUSH-A-BYE, BABY

Hush-a-bye, baby,
    Daddy is near;
Mamma is a lady,
    And that 's very clear.

BIRDS OF A FEATHER

Birds of a feather flock together,

And so will pigs and swine;

Rats and mice will have their choice,

And so will I have mine.

COCK-A-DOODLE-DO

Oh, my pretty cock! Oh, my handsome cock!

I pray you, do not crow before day,

And your comb shall be made of the very beaten gold,

And your wings of the silver so gray.

HUSH, BABY, MY DOLLY

Hush, baby, my dolly, I pray you don't cry,

And I'll give you some bread and some milk by and by;

Or perhaps you like custard, or maybe a tart,

Then to either you're welcome, with all my heart.

I HAD A LITTLE PONY

HAD a little pony
His name was Dapple-Grey,
I lent him to a lady,
To ride a mile away.
She whipped him, she lashed him,
She rode him through the mire;
I would not lend my pony now
For all the lady's hire.

SNAIL

Snail, snail, come out of
your hole,
Or else I 'll beat you as
black as a coal.
Snail, snail, put out your
horns,
Here comes a thief to pull
down your walls.

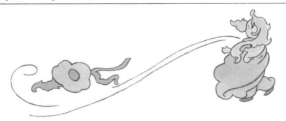

MY LADY WIND

My lady Wind, my lady Wind,
Went round about the house to find
    A chink to get her foot in:
She tried the keyhole in the door,
She tried the crevice in the floor,
    And drove the chimney soot in.

And then one night, when it was dark,
She blew up such a tiny spark,
    That all the house was pothered:
From it she raised up such a flame,
As flamed away to Belting Lane,
    And White Cross folks were smothered.

And thus when once, my little dears,
A whisper reaches itching ears,
    The same will come, you'll find:
Take my advice, restrain the tongue,
Remember what old nurse has sung
    Of busy lady Wind!

LITTLE JENNY WREN

As little Jenny Wren
    Was sitting by the shed,
She waggled with her tail,
    And nodded with her head.

She waggled with her tail,
    And nodded with her head,
As little Jenny Wren
    Was sitting by the shed.

POOR ROBIN

The north wind doth blow,
    And we shall have snow,
And what will poor Robin do
    then?
        Poor thing!

He'll sit in a barn,
    And to keep himself warm
Will hide his head under his
    wing.
        Poor thing!